Sounds of
The
Pacific Northwest

Written By Anna Hill

Illustrated By Dru Hill

A & D Hill
CHILDREN'S BOOKS

Shhhhhh...

Let's listen to the sounds
of the Pacific Northwest...

Chirp Chirp

Squeaks the Sea Otter,
As he plays within the waves.
He searches through the coastal rocks,
For the little crabs he craves.

SQUIRT SQUIRT

Splashes the Geoduck,
When its siphon shoots out water.
It burrows under the cold beach clay,
As the day grows hotter.

HOOOOONK

Shrieks the Canadian Goose,
As he flaps his big brown wings.
It's a warning to give space,
For his newly hatched goslings.

SLUUUURP

Slimes the Banana Slug,
Across the forest floor.
His tentacles are probing,
For yummy leaves that he adores.

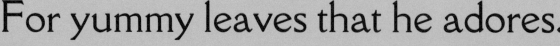

Munch Munch

Chomps the Beaver,
As his big teeth fell a tree.
He builds a dam upriver,
With all the tree's debris.

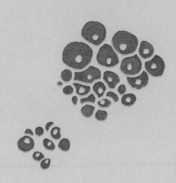

Blub Blub

Says the Salmon,
When her migration has begun.
Her hard swim up the river,
Is called the salmon run.

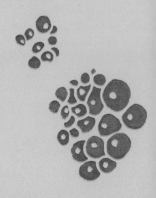

SCREEECH

Cries the Bald Eagle,
From within her great big nest.
She guards her baby eaglet,
So he can get some rest.

Roooar

Calls the Black Bear,
Full of fishes that he ate.
When winter comes, he'll find his den,
So he can hibernate.

Whooo Whooo

Sings the Orca Whale,
Within the Puget Sound.
She calls beneath the water,
For her pod to gather round.

YOOOOOWL

Cries the Cougar,
As she prowls in the night.
She's speaking to her little cubs,
Who are hiding out of sight.

SPLASH

Plunges the Blue Heron,
Into the ocean pool.
She uses her long bill,
As her nimble fishing tool.

Yawwwn

The animals are headed,
To their burrows, dens, and nests.
It's time to say "goodnight",
So we all can get some rest.
Shhhhhh...

With love for all our children
- Anna & Dru

This book was a collaborative effort between mother and daughter. Dru has a BA of Fine Arts and a Masters in Education. Her artwork has been shown in galleries across the US. Anna is a mother of two, whose short stories have been published by Havok Publishing and in the Retelling Her World Anthology.

We hope you enjoyed reading this book as much as we enjoyed creating it! We would love to hear from you in an Amazon review! Sounds of The Desert is currently available on Amazon. And stay tuned for our next book, Sounds of Magical Creatures.

Made in the USA
Columbia, SC
03 August 2024

39944151R00018